This book belongs to:

_____

For Faith Ruby who isn't scared of bears. J.J.
For Martha: may your bears be ever cute and fluffy. L.C.

First published in Great Britain in 2010 by Andersen Press Ltd.,
20 Vauxhall Bridge Road, London SW1V 2SA.
Published in Australia by Random House Australia Pty.,
Level 3, 100 Pacific Highway, North Sydney, NSW 2060.
Text copyright © Julia Jarman, 2010.
Illustration copyright © Lynne Chapman, 2010.
The rights of Julia Jarman and Lynne Chapman to be identified
as the author and illustrator of this work have been asserted by them
in accordance with the Copyright, Designs and Patents Act, 1988.
All rights reserved.
Colour separated in Switzerland by Photolitho AG, Zürich.
Printed and bound in Singapore by Tien Wah Press.

10   9   8   7   6   5   4   3   2   1

British Library Cataloguing in Publication Data available.
ISBN 978 1 84939 005 7 (hbk)
ISBN 978 1 84939 028 6 (pbk)
This book has been printed on acid-free paper

Bears on the Stairs

Julia Jarman

Lynne Chapman

ANDERSEN PRESS

There are bears on the stairs.
That's why I don't like going to bed.
It's the bears on the stairs.

On the bottom step there's a little one, but he's very fierce and growly.

Mummy doesn't believe me.

In the middle there's a fat one with **big**, biffy paws. Mummy says there isn't.

At the top there's a **huge** one.
He's right outside my bedroom door so I can't go in.

You should see his teeth.

Mummy says it's my imagination and "Have you cleaned your teeth? It's past your bedtime. Go on. Upstairs."

The little one says I can pass, if I give him a chocolate biscuit.

The middle one says I've got
to get him a drink of milk.

The big one says,
"NO WAY. Even if you give
me a drink and a biscuit
and a whole bar of
chocolate you
CANNOT
come
upstairs."

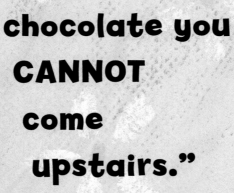

Mummy still doesn't believe me.

Nor does Daddy.

When Mummy and Daddy come upstairs with me, the bears hide.

BUT . . .

. . . I bet my bears will get them on the way down!

Other books you might enjoy:

9781849390576

9781842709702

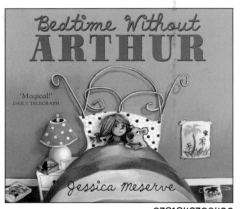

9781842709436

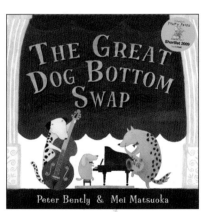

9781842709887

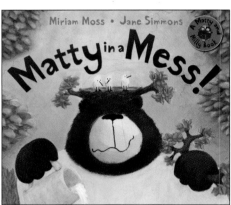

9781842709467